SAVING OSCAR

June Crebbin was a primary school teacher before taking early retirement to concentrate on her writing. She is the author of a number of books for children, including the first story about Merryfield Hall Riding School, *Jumping Beany*, as well as several picture books for younger children. A frequent visitor to primary schools to give readings, talks and workshops, June lives in Leicestershire, where she enjoys horse riding as often as possible!

Another Merryfield Hall Riding School book

Jumping Beany

More books by the same author

The Curse of the Skull
The Dragon Test
Emmelina and the Monster
Hal the Highwayman
Horse Tales
No Tights for George!
Tarquin the Wonder Horse

Merryfield Hall · Riding School ·

Saving Oscar

June Crebbin

WALKER
BOOKS

First published 2007 by Walker Books Ltd
87 Vauxhall Walk, London SE11 5HJ

2 4 6 8 10 9 7 5 3

Text © 2007 June Crebbin
Cover photograph © Juniors Bildarchiv/Alamy

The right of June Crebbin to be identified as author
of this work has been asserted by her in accordance
with the Copyright, Designs and Patents Act 1988

This book has been typeset in Stempel Schneidler

Printed in Great Britain by J. H. Haynes & Co. Ltd

British Library Cataloguing in Publication Data:
a catalogue record for this book
is available from the British Library

ISBN 978-1-4063-0199-1

www.walkerbooks.co.uk

For Jordan Carduss

With special thanks to Jane and Gail

Amber fell in love with Oscar the moment she saw him. That is, the moment she saw him properly. The first time she set eyes on him, she was almost blinded with anger at what was happening.

It was a day Amber had been looking forward to for months. The first day of the summer Pony Camp at Merryfield Hall Riding School. The hall itself was now a very posh hotel with livery stables where horse and pony owners could keep their mounts. The riding school was completely separate with its own stables and, in the summer, tents!

Amber couldn't wait. Five whole days of riding her favourite pony, Beany!

But the day started badly.

"How come," said Amber, thumping her rucksack through the tent flap and crawling in after it, "we've been landed with Donna?"

Molly crawled in after her. "Don't ask me. I didn't choose her. I just put you on the booking form."

"But you know we have to have three to a tent!" said Amber. "Jen's filled in the gap. You were supposed to put down two friends."

"Oh," said Molly. "I didn't think. Sorry." She sat back on her heels. "I wonder if any-one chose Donna," she said. She couldn't imagine why they would. Donna was so bossy and full of herself.

Amber picked up her hat. "Come on," she said. "We can sort this lot out later." She couldn't wait to start riding.

Molly followed Amber to the indoor arena.

Jen, their instructor, was sorting everyone into groups.

"No sign of Donna," murmured Amber, looking round.

"You mean...?" said Molly.

"Maybe she's not coming," said Amber. "You know what her family's like. They've probably gone to Barbados!" She grinned. "Cross everything!"

The first session was grooming. Jen checked that everyone knew which pony they'd be riding for the week. Molly went off happily to Feather. She always rode Feather. He was old and slow, but that's how Molly liked it.

Amber was last. "You'll be riding Polka," said Jen.

"Who's riding Beany?" said Amber. It was bound to be Donna.

"I'm afraid Beany's been sold," said Jen. "Do you remember Martin, who used to come on Pony Days?"

Amber couldn't think straight. She shook her head.

"Well, he's bought Beany," said Jen. "I know you'll miss him. But you like Polka, don't you?" She smiled. "He's fun, isn't he?"

Amber nodded, but the lump in her throat prevented her from speaking.

"Off you go then," said Jen.

Amber walked away. All those times when Donna had ridden Beany, she'd known it would be her turn next, but now...

She found Polka and set to work. She brushed him vigorously, almost viciously, worrying at bits of mud long after they'd disappeared. She'd looked forward so much to this week. But it had always involved Beany. Now she would never ride him again. She couldn't take it in.

Molly appeared. "Why aren't you riding Beany?" she said.

Amber turned away. "Tell you later."

She concentrated on getting the bit into

Polka's mouth. He never wanted to leave his hay-net.

One of the older girls came by, leading a big chestnut mare. "Your group's on," she said. "Jen's waiting."

"Don't go without me," wailed Molly, rushing off to fetch Feather. By the time they arrived at the arena, the lesson had started. The ponies were walking around the arena, one behind the other, stepping out briskly.

Jen let Amber and Molly in and told them to join the end of the ride. "You'll have to work at being on time," she said.

Amber pushed Polka forwards with her calves, thrusting her heels well down in the stirrups.

"Push Feather on, Molly," called Jen. "He's lagging behind."

"Can we do canter pick-up?" yelled Jack, who was riding Rocket Roger as usual.

Jen agreed. "But first I'd like to see what

your sitting trot is like," she said.

Amber forced herself to concentrate. Polka was unpredictable. If he trotted too fast, she bounced about in the saddle; if she slowed him down, he took that as a signal to walk. It was hard getting just the right amount of speed.

"Well done!" called Jen. "Now, rising trot everyone. Jack, forward to canter!"

"Is canter pick-up where we—" hissed Molly from behind Amber.

"Just watch the others," called Jen. "You'll soon remember."

Jack, who was at the head of the ride, set off at a canter around the arena. Everyone else carried on trotting.

"Make sure you're ready!" called Jen to Lydia, who was second in line. "As soon as Jack draws level, you canter with him."

"I know!" yelled Lydia. She shortened her reins on Silver. Off they went, as soon as Jack arrived. Then Jack joined the end of the ride and Lydia cantered on and picked up the third rider, and so on.

Polka was getting excited. He kept spinning round on the spot.

"Mind me," said Molly, backing out of the way.

"Be ready!" cried Amber to Molly, as she flew off on her turn.

Molly was ready, but when Amber and Polka dropped off at the end of their canter, Feather decided he'd had enough and he stopped too.

Just then a voice called from outside the arena. "Jen, can I come in?"

Amber's heart sank. So it was going to happen. A whole week of Donna in their tent, listening to their conversations, spreading her expensive belongings all over their space.

"Sorry I'm late," called Donna. "Sparkle didn't like his new trailer, did you, darling?"

Sparkle?

Someone opened the gate. Into the arena danced the most exquisite pony Amber had ever seen. Dapple grey with a silky, dark grey mane and tail, an intelligent head, perfectly shaped legs and a slender, but not skinny, body.

Everyone gasped.

"Is he yours?" asked Jack.

Donna nodded. "Just got him yesterday," she smirked.

Jen helped her mount up. "Let Sparkle join in quietly," she said. "He's bound to feel a bit strange at first in a new place."

Donna rode past Amber. "Not riding Beany?" she said. "Oh dear."

Of course, Donna knew all about Beany being sold.

"We thought about getting him for me," she insisted on telling Amber at lunchtime. "But then we heard about Sparkle." She reeled off all the shows Sparkle had been in and how many cups he'd won. "He's ace at jumping," she said. "You'll see."

Amber did see. Jen took them out to the cross-country field in the afternoon. The jumps weren't high but they were fixed so you had to think carefully about what you were doing. Jen took them over each jump in turn to start with, pointing out how to approach it, how to get a good line. Then they tackled three, one after the other, then the whole course, eight jumps in all.

Polka ran out at the ditch. Sparkle cleared everything.

"Isn't he wonderful?" cried Donna. She went on and on. "He's only staying here this week because of Pony Camp. Then he's going to be at the livery stables up at the hall." She was still going on while they were getting ready to go to the pub in nearby Thornby village for their evening meal.

There wasn't a lot of room in the tent now that Donna had arrived. For one thing, she had brought a suitcase whereas everyone else had brought rucksacks. The suitcase was filled, as Amber had known it would be, with expensive fleeces, classy jodhpurs, snazzy tops, cute trousers – and sweets. Overflowing not just with small packets of sweets like most people, but with big bags of them and family-size sacks of chocolate bars.

"Have one," she invited airily, spilling them out. "I've got loads."

"Thanks," said Molly, reaching out eagerly.

Amber scowled. She turned her back, pulled on a top and a pair of jeans and went outside to play on the trampoline until it was time to go.

"Some friend you are," Amber told Molly as they walked down the lane.

"Well, I was hungry – and Donna was only trying to be nice," said Molly.

Amber snorted. "I wouldn't take one of her sweets if it was the last sweet on earth," she said.

Molly sighed. It was going to be a difficult week.

On the way back to the stables after their meal, they passed the village playground.

"Can we?" asked Jack. "We've brought a ball."

Mel, who was in charge along with her friend Sam, saw the possibility of a chat.

"Why not?" she said.

Cheering, everyone hurtled into the play area. Some took over the football pitch. Others scattered about in groups, idly swinging and chatting or balancing on logs arranged in the shape of a dinosaur. Mel and Sam settled themselves on the bench.

"Let's go on the see-saw," said Molly.

"No, thanks," said Amber.

She didn't want to do anything. This was meant to have been the week to end all weeks. No school. No homework. Nobody telling her what to do. Just riding Beany, looking after him, having fun.

All spoilt.

She wandered up to the football pitch.

"Want to play?" yelled Jack.

Amber smiled. She was about to say yes, when something attracted her attention a couple of fields away.

"No, thanks," she said.

Amber stood on the fence in order to see.

There was a pony. It galloped into view, stopped, threw up its head, whinnied loudly and galloped on again. There was something about the way it moved. Not a free galloping, the way ponies normally do, kicking up their heels for the sheer fun of it. This pony kept stopping. When it stopped, it seemed to be watching. It seemed to be waiting.

Amber realized she couldn't see the whole field. One of the sides was out of view behind a small building and it was this side the pony watched; this side it galloped away from. In a lull in the football game, Amber heard shouting, saw something that appalled her, and was over the fence running, running.

As she reached the pony's field, she could see exactly what was happening.

A gang of boys was throwing stones. Another boy stood not far off, watching.

"Stop it!" Amber shouted.

Either the boys didn't hear or they chose

to ignore her. They were good shots. Stones flew through the air and hit the pony time after time, sending it into a frenzy.

Amber climbed over the fence and ran across the field towards them.

"Don't!" she cried. "You'll hurt it."

The boys paused. Then, deliberately, one of them stooped, picked up a stone, raised his arm – and turned to face her.

"Do you want some then?" he asked.

Amber backed away. "Don't be silly," she said. "It's dangerous."

The boys fell about laughing. Then the one with the stone turned and threw it, expertly. It caught the pony's ear.

"Please don't," begged Amber. "You could kill him."

The boys thought this was even funnier.

"That'll save Bill a job then," one of them spluttered. He drew his finger slowly across his throat. "Dead meat tomorrow," he said. "Dog meat! Poor old Oscar!"

They collapsed with laughter again.

"I don't believe you!" shouted Amber.

The boy shrugged. "First thing tomorrow," he said.

"Rescue?" said Molly when, later, Amber told her about the pony. "What do you mean – rescue?"

"Sshh," warned Amber. They were walking down the lane back to the stables. She took hold of Molly's arm. "Stay behind a bit," she said. "We've got to make plans and I don't want anyone else to hear."

By anyone, Molly guessed she mostly meant Donna.

"We have to rescue that pony," began Amber.

"What's it like?" interrupted Molly.

"I don't know," said Amber. "I didn't have

time to have a proper look. I know he's called Oscar…"

"That's a nice name," said Molly.

"Those boys didn't think so," said Amber. "They were laughing at it." She shuddered. They'd made fun of her too, imitating her voice, saying things like, "Oooh – it's dangerous!" and "Aaah – poor little pony!"

"Anyway," continued Amber, "that pony is going to be killed tomorrow unless we do something about it tonight."

"You mean, tell Jen about it when we get back," said Molly.

"We could do that," Amber agreed, "but she probably won't do anything until tomorrow and by then it'll be too late."

"What, then?"

Amber outlined her plan.

Molly was horrified. "We can't!" she said. "We're not even allowed to go to the village shop without permission, let alone go wandering off on our own in the middle of the night to steal a pony!"

"Well, of course, if you want an innocent creature's death on your conscience," said Amber, "that's up to you."

Molly stared at her. "I didn't say I wouldn't do it," she said. "I'd just rather we told Jen."

"We will," promised Amber. "Tomorrow. But we must get Oscar out of that field tonight."

It was past midnight before the campsite was quiet, though Mel and Sam had been trying to get everyone into their tents since ten o'clock. No one had felt sleepy. It was too exciting being outside playing games, fooling about.

During the evening, Amber unpacked her belongings and filled her rucksack instead with a few "borrowed" items from the stables. She added her own torch and Molly's.

"It's my dad's car torch," said Molly.

"Much better than mine," said Amber.

Molly began to feel excited. After all, what they were doing wasn't wrong. They were saving an innocent creature.

She and Amber managed to get into their sleeping bags fully dressed while Donna was in the washrooms. They pretended to be asleep when she came back. Molly almost dozed off, she was so tired, but suddenly she felt a prod. She opened her eyes to see Amber with a finger on her lips.

Donna was asleep.

Cautiously, they eased themselves out of their sleeping bags, slid through the tent flap and stepped out into the warm night.

It was eerie going down the lane to the village. Although there was a full moon, the trees lining each side met overhead, making a leafy tunnel. In daylight, it was pleasant and shady. At night, it was spooky – branches moving restlessly above them, creaking.

Amber and Molly were glad to reach the main street where the sky was clear. They switched off their torches, hurried through the playground and climbed the fence on the other side of the football pitch.

As they crossed the next field, they could see the pony.

"What if he bites?" whispered Molly. "Or kicks?"

She wasn't too keen on catching ponies at the best of times.

Amber shrugged. "Cross everything!" she said.

They climbed over the fence into the pony's field. He looked up.

That was when Amber saw him properly for the first time. He was a rich chestnut brown with a creamy mane and tail, like a Palomino. He had a blaze of white down his face and soft brown eyes. He didn't look old or ill or anything. Why would anyone want to kill him?

Amber approached him quietly, calling his name. Oscar watched as she drew closer. Amber could tell he was poised ready to take off in an instant, but she could also see he was interested in the bucket she was carrying. As soon as she was close enough, she offered it to him. He lowered his head. Quietly, she slipped the lead-rope round his neck, talking to him all the time, reassuring him. Then she eased the head-collar over his ears.

Molly was waiting at the gate. It creaked a bit as she opened it.

"Sshh!" warned Amber.

"I can't help it," said Molly.

"Don't shut it," hissed Amber. "We don't want to wake the whole village."

Molly pulled a face. "I wasn't going to," she muttered.

They hadn't bargained for the amount of noise one pony's hooves could make on the road. Amber expected heads to pop out of windows any minute. But she saw no one.

All the same, she had the weirdest feeling they were being watched. Twice she stopped to look behind her, and once, as they passed Thornby Manor, she found herself looking up; but only the blank windows looked back.

At the edge of the village, past the church, they came to the field where the riding-school ponies were turned out each night.

"They might not like him," said Molly.

Amber nodded. "It's a risk we have to take," she said. She knew perfectly well that in normal circumstances you never sent a new pony into a field full of ponies who were used to each other. You put it in the next field and let them make friends over the hedge first. But these weren't normal circumstances.

"Now or never," said Amber. Molly opened the gate and Amber led Oscar in. At once some ponies galloped over to see what was happening.

"Good luck, Oscar," Amber whispered. She slipped off the head-collar and got out of the way. There was no kicking but there was a good deal of squealing and nibbling before the ponies went their separate ways again, grazing peacefully.

"Doesn't Oscar look happy?" said Molly, as they secured the gate. "I'm glad we rescued him."

Amber nodded. For the time being, Oscar was safe.

"And no one saw us," said Molly.

About that, Amber wasn't so sure.

Amber had meant it when she promised Molly they'd tell Jen. But when she woke the following morning, she began to have doubts. Jen would find out about Oscar anyway, as soon as they fetched the ponies in from the field.

Amber tried to think what would happen.

If they didn't say anything, no one would know where Oscar had come from. And – Amber sat up – if Jen didn't know where he'd come from, *she couldn't send him back*.

That was the important thing.

Jen might notify the police or send for

the RSPCA, but either way, Oscar would still be safe.

The more Amber thought about it, the more convinced she became. There was absolutely no need to say anything.

She told Molly over breakfast. "So when Oscar is discovered, you just have to keep quiet," she warned.

"Oh, I will," said Molly.

They set off with Mel and the others to the pony field straight after breakfast. Mel noticed Oscar as soon as they arrived.

"Where did he come from?" she said, opening the gate. "Stay back all of you. I'll catch him. He might bite."

"He doesn't," said Molly.

Everyone looked at her. Molly went red.

"How do you know?" asked Mel.

"She doesn't," said Amber, quickly. "But, honestly, look at him. You can tell butter wouldn't melt in his mouth. He's so sweet."

"Maybe," said Mel. "All the same." She set

off importantly across the field.

Oscar was no trouble. He even nosed around Mel's pockets while she popped on a head-collar.

"He's really friendly," said Lydia.

Amber shot Molly a warning glance not to say another word. But Molly was fully occupied catching Feather.

Someone dashed off to fetch another head-collar, and eventually they all arrived back at the stables.

Amber saw Oscar being put in an empty stable. She saw Mel going off in the direction of the office, but then she had to get Polka tacked up. Their group was in the arena first.

"Lydia says we're doing 'Chase me, Charlie'," said Molly, arriving with Feather. "Is that where—"

"Jen'll tell you," said Amber, struggling to fasten Polka's girth. He would keep blowing his tummy out.

"She won't," said Lydia, passing by with Silver. "Kate's taking us."

"Why?" said Molly. "Where's Jen?"

Lydia stopped. "She's had to go somewhere. Something to do with her mother being ill I think."

Molly and Amber exchanged glances. So they couldn't tell Jen about rescuing Oscar even if they wanted to.

"Oh and it's jumping," said Lydia over her shoulder as she moved away. "Where it gets higher and higher."

"Oh dear," said Molly.

Amber liked "Chase me, Charlie". Only two jumps were involved, a practice jump and the real one, which started off quite low so that everyone had a chance, then got higher and higher. You had to "keep the pot boiling", chasing the person in front of you the minute they were over the practice jump. As soon as you knocked the pole off the real jump, you were eliminated and the winner was the person who jumped the highest.

First they warmed up. They practised transitions, going smoothly from walk to trot, then smoothly back to walk again. They worked on sitting trot without stirrups.

Much easier than with them, thought Amber, sitting deep in the saddle and dangling her legs as low as she could.

"Are you taking us all week?" Jack asked Kate, trying to hold Roger to a steady trot.

"Probably," said Kate. "Until Jen gets back anyway."

They were all used to Kate. She was an instructor who often took over if Jen was in a meeting or delayed for some reason. She was stricter than Jen. She didn't allow chatting as they rode.

"Feet back in the stirrups," she called. "Test your girths."

The competition began.

Amber tried to concentrate. She wanted to win. She always wanted to win, but this week

34

it was even more important. Every day during Pony Camp points were awarded for the first three places in each activity and the overall winner at the end of the week received the Merryfield Cup with the name of the rider and pony engraved on it.

Amber had thought about it so often – imagine taking a cup home! But now all she could think about was Oscar. She hoped he was all right.

"Well done, Donna!" said Kate, as Sparkle jumped the highest. "Your new pony's a bit of a star, isn't he?"

Amber put Polka away and untacked him. As soon as the others had gone over to the house for drinks, she checked that Oscar was still in the stable where she'd last seen him and hurried across to the office.

Carol was working at the computer. Amber studied the noticeboard.

Eventually Carol looked up. "Shouldn't you be having your break?" she said. She never liked pony campers cluttering up her office.

"I was just wondering if there was any news about the pony that was found," said Amber.

Carol turned back to the computer. "Not that I know," she said.

Amber left.

At lunchtime Oscar was still in the stable. And he was still there when they all set off to the village for their evening meal. On the way, Amber quizzed Mel and Sam. But they knew nothing. Or they weren't saying.

"I can't understand it," said Amber, drawing Molly to one side. "No one seems to know anything."

"Well, that's good, isn't it?" said Molly. "He's safe where he is."

Amber felt uneasy. Surely someone should have reported him missing by now.

Two men were standing chatting at the bar as the pony campers passed through on their way to the side room where they ate their meal.

Amber caught only a few words but she knew at once what they were talking about. "I'll catch you up," she whispered to Molly. She picked up a menu and pretended to read it.

"Up at the manor," one man was saying. "That pony. It's a crying shame. Bill should have taken it today. But someone nicked it!"

The other man laughed. "In the nick of time you could say!"

"It's at the riding school," said the barman. "At least that's what I heard." He pulled a pint for a customer. "Going tomorrow, though."

Amber drew in her breath. So Oscar belonged to the family who lived at Thornby Manor. Somehow his owner had been traced. At the thought of the owner, Amber felt her blood boil. What sort of person would want to get rid of a perfectly healthy, beautiful pony?

During the meal, Amber thought hard. For the first time, she wished she could tell Jen. She was sure if she explained it properly, Jen would be on their side; would see what a lovely pony he was, and want to save him too.

But it was no use wishing. Jen wasn't there. Amber had to decide what to do now.

When they got back to their tent, Amber told Molly about the conversation she had overheard in the pub.

"So we have to move him again," said Amber. "Tonight."

Molly was horrified. "Oh, no," she said. "I just can't." She had been so relieved when Amber had decided they needn't say anything about rescuing Oscar.

Amber shrugged. "Fine. If that's how you feel, I'll do it without you."

Molly hated it when Amber fell out with her.

"If we told someone—" she began.

"Who?" demanded Amber. "Who could

we trust? Think about it. He's been here all day and no one's made any effort to save him. Have they?"

Molly shook her head.

"So are you going to help me or not?" said Amber.

"Where would we move him to?" said Molly.

Amber had thought about that. Ponies weren't like thimbles to be hidden behind cushions or popped under carpets. Ponies needed space, and food, and shelter.

"That," said Amber, "depends on Donna."

"You mean you stole him!" said Donna, when Amber told her how she and Molly had rescued Oscar the night before.

"Only because of what was going to happen," said Molly.

Donna grinned smugly. "I knew you two were up to something," she said.

Amber looked at her suspiciously. "Did you follow us?"

"Of course not," said Donna.

"Well, someone did," said Amber. "Anyway, the reason I'm telling you all this is" – she took a deep breath – "we need your help."

Donna couldn't disguise her surprise. "Me?"

"You said that Sparkle is going to the livery stables," said Amber, ignoring her. "And he's only staying here this week because of Pony Camp?"

Donna nodded.

"So," continued Amber, "does that mean that right now Sparkle's stable is empty?"

Donna agreed. "But I don't want Sparkle to go there yet—" She broke off as Amber interrupted.

"Not Sparkle. Oscar."

Light dawned. "Oh," said Donna. "You mean..."

If they could hide Oscar even for a few days, explained Amber, there'd be a chance of saving him – Jen might be back by then. Whereas if he stayed where he was...

"It costs money, you know," said Donna. "They don't live rent-free."

"I'll pay you back," said Amber. "Now, do

41

you know the phone number of the livery stables?"

Donna took out her mobile. "It's already in my phone," she said. "But there won't be anyone there now."

"Exactly!" said Amber. "So you don't need to talk to anyone. Just leave a message."

Amber went over the details. Donna was to say there'd been a change of plan and that she'd like to bring her pony to his new home tomorrow.

"They've never seen Sparkle, have they?" said Amber.

Donna shook her head.

"So no one will know it's not him," said Amber. "We'll have to do it very early in the morning though, so that no one sees us taking Oscar from here."

"I'd better stay," said Molly, "in case anyone asks where you are." She broke off. "Of course I won't tell them," she added.

Donna rang the livery stables. Suddenly

she put her hand over the mouthpiece. "Someone's answered!"

"Give them the message!" said Amber.

Within seconds Donna clapped her hand over the phone again. "They want my mum's number!"

"Make one up," said Amber. "Better still..." She took the mobile. "Hello," she said in her poshest grown-up voice. "Yes, that's correct. Thank you so much." She rang off.

Donna giggled.

"I wouldn't like to be in your shoes when your mum finds out," said Molly.

Donna shrugged. "By then," she said, "I'll be famous. My picture will be in all the papers – GIRL SAVES PONY – and she'll be so proud of me, it won't matter."

"That's not why we're doing it," said Molly.

"*You* are not doing it at all," Donna reminded her.

* * *

Promptly at five o'clock the following morning, Amber's alarm went off. She hadn't slept much and she was already awake and dressed. If only the plan would work. If only they could keep Oscar hidden.

Amazingly, everything went smoothly. By six o'clock, Oscar was settled in his new home; Amber and Donna were back at camp; no one had seen them.

Molly was awake. "Was it all right?"

"Of course," said Donna.

Amber took herself off to the washrooms. As long as Jen came back before the end of the week, before Sparkle had to be delivered to his new home, all would be well.

She began to look forward to the day's events. First, the "turn-out" competition. You had one hour in which to groom your pony to perfection. You were allowed to use the wash-box, which was just as well as Polka had two white socks, usually dirty grey after being in the field all night. You could plait your pony's mane and tail. You could oil his hooves.

Amber worked quickly. By ten o'clock Polka's speckled, roan coat shone. Amber picked out his feet, applied hoof oil to the bottom of them and to his hooves – she knew Kate would look for details like that – and started on his mane.

It was hopeless. Polka's hair was so coarse and wiry, it kept springing out of the plait in ugly tufts, no matter how carefully Amber tried to work it in. She decided to brush it out instead. She brushed Polka's tail until it flowed. Then, with a few minutes left, she bathed his eyes and nostrils gently but thoroughly.

At half past ten all the ponies were led to the outdoor arena, paraded round and lined up. Kate inspected. Amber held her breath. Molly had done really well with Feather. His mane was neatly plaited and she'd put a french plait in his tail. Amber couldn't help feeling envious. It looked very striking.

Kate was enthusiastic about everyone's efforts. She complimented Amber on her attention to detail and approved her decision not to plait.

But it was Sparkle who won.

"Doesn't he look lovely?" said Molly, who was over the moon at coming second.

"He's a show pony," said Amber.

Kate reminded them the week wasn't over yet. "Don't forget 'Top Score' this afternoon!" she said. "That's a really good opportunity to earn points!"

"Is that where—" began Molly. "No, don't tell me. I know. It's where every jump has points, the more difficult the jump, the higher the score, and you only have one minute to do it!"

"And?" said Amber.

"What?"

"You're not supposed to jump only the easy ones!"

"The rules say you can do any jumps you like and that's what I do," said Molly.

"You won't win!" said Amber.

She had a pretty good idea who would.

But she was wrong.

As soon as the competition started, Amber knew she was in with a chance. Polka was enjoying himself. In the practice rounds, she worked out her plan. If she chose four moderate jumps, that would give her a reasonable number of points, but if she chose the most difficult one, the spread, and just a couple of others, that would earn far more. The spread carried fifty points.

Amber went for it. Her top score of eighty-five beat Jack, who flew round but didn't tackle the spread. Donna came third.

"Sparkle's not used to being rushed," said Donna.

"You were ace!" said Molly, as she and Amber put their ponies away.

"Thanks," said Amber. She felt happier than she'd been all week. The more the day wore on, the more she relaxed.

That night she slept soundly.

The following morning Molly had to shake Amber awake.

"Come on," she said. "It's the hack today."

Kate called them all together before they tacked up. "Just a quick chat," she said, "about the sort of things I'll be looking for when we're out on our ride. Any ideas?"

"Consideration," said Jack. "Being polite to other road users."

Kate nodded.

"Staying in line," suggested Lydia.

"Not racing when we canter," said Molly. She hated going fast.

"I'm not sure I'll be able to hold Sparkle

back," said Donna. "I'd better be at the front."

Amber wasn't the only one who groaned.

By ten o'clock, everyone was ready to set off. Kate was at the head, Mel halfway along the line and Sam at the back.

"If anyone has a problem," said Kate, "shout to whoever's nearest."

Molly gripped Feather's reins. She was riding last, just in front of Sam. "I'm really nervous," she said.

"You'll be fine," said Amber, who was in front of her.

Polka was excited. His ears were pricked. He stepped out eagerly as they trotted up the lane. But he eased back when Amber drew him into the side as a car approached. Amber remembered to thank the driver.

At the end of the lane, they turned down a stony path.

"Oh, no," said Molly. "We're going across the brook."

"Feather likes paddling!" said Amber.

Suddenly, the line came to a stop.

Someone was having trouble up ahead.

"It's Sparkle," said Sam, standing up in her stirrups to see. "He doesn't want to go in the water." She went to investigate.

"I hope she won't be long," said Molly.

Amber didn't mind waiting. The sun was shining. It was a lovely day for a hack. Oscar was not only safe but being looked after.

A slight noise in the hedge caught her attention. A boy was sitting on a stile. A bike, presumably his, lay on its side nearby. He was staring at her.

Amber felt her stomach lurch. Was he one of the gang that had thrown stones? She looked away.

At that moment the line moved forward. Sam came back to her place, bringing Donna with her.

"You come after me," Sam told Donna. "Sparkle will follow if he thinks he's going to get left behind."

Amber rode forward, across the brook, up the steep bank on the far side and waited with the others. She glanced back. No sign of the boy. Had she imagined him staring at her?

There was no time to think further, as Molly appeared, followed by Sam and then Donna.

But Amber felt unsettled.

They cantered up the hill at the edge of the next field.

"Stay in line," called Kate, but hardly had they started before Donna and Sparkle streaked past.

There were two more canters before they reached a neighbouring village. Amber loved trotting up the hill past the quiet cottages, the only sound that of hooves striking the road in rhythm.

As they turned down the lane out of the village, Amber was aware of the boy again. He was riding his bike, about to draw level with her. But a tractor approached. The riders slowed to a walk and drew in to the side.

The boy quickly cycled on.

Amber was sure he had been about to speak.

"Do we have any more canters?" called Molly.

"Don't know!" yelled Amber, watching the boy disappear round the bend in the road, pedalling fast.

"One more," said Sam, "and you don't have to keep in line."

"Oh dear," said Molly.

It was exciting to see everyone spread across the field in the last canter. Amber let Polka move on a bit. Sam was keeping Molly company at the back.

They drew up breathless at the gate. Molly was glowing. "I loved it!" she said, patting Feather's neck. "That was great!"

Amber laughed.

The boy, the same boy, was holding the

gate open. Everyone thanked him as they went through.

As Amber passed, he spoke, quite low. Amber thought he said: "Can you come to Thornby Manor?" She leant down to fiddle with her stirrup, and the boy said it again. This time Amber was sure.

She rode on. After a moment she glanced behind. The boy had closed the gate and was picking up his bike.

"He fancies you!" said Sam. "He's been following us all the way round."

Amber blushed. She pushed Polka on to catch up with the others, her mind buzzing. Who was he? Was he something to do with Oscar? Even if she tried to do what he asked, how could she get away from the camp? She could hardly visit him in the middle of the night!

Kate set a brisk pace back to the stables, only slowing to a walk when they reached the village and went past the church, round by the shop and along the main street.

As they clattered into the yard, a pony lifted its head to look out of its stable, a pony with a white blaze down his face and soft brown eyes...

Amber stared in disbelief. How on earth?

Mel came to take Sparkle. "Kate wants a word," she told Donna.

Amber untacked Polka, knowing it was her fault Donna was in trouble. She hung around the stables, waiting, until Mel noticed and told her to go for lunch.

"Swimming this afternoon," she said. "Hurry up. The coach comes at two."

Amber had forgotten about swimming. "I'm waiting for Donna," she said.

"Donna went across ages ago," said Mel.

Amber ran over to the house, grabbed

some sandwiches and an apple and found Donna, apparently without a care in the world, with Molly.

"What happened?" demanded Amber.

It appeared that Donna's mother had called in at the livery stables, just by chance, to sort out something or other before Sparkle arrived—

"And was told Sparkle had already arrived!" interrupted Molly. "Only of course it wasn't, it was—"

"Oscar," said Amber. "But what about the phone call?"

"Easy," said Donna. "Couldn't have been me, my mobile's not working. Needs charging."

"But it was working..."

"Must have been someone playing a trick on me," said Donna, ignoring her. "There are some funny people about."

Molly giggled. Donna stood up. "Anyway, no one knows anything. Relax. There's nothing to worry about."

Except, thought Amber, that Oscar is back here. She was sure someone at the manor would have been informed by now.

"Come on, Molly," said Donna. "Swimming, remember."

"Can't wait!" said Molly, jumping up.

Everyone was flying about, changing into shorts, collecting swimming gear.

Amber went to find Kate.

"I don't feel well," she said. "Is it all right if I stay here?"

Kate was concerned, but Amber assured her it was just a headache. "I'll lie down in the shade, shall I?" she said.

"Good idea," said Kate. "Carol's in the office if you need her, and Sam's here."

The coach rolled off down the lane.

Amber found a shady spot and sat down. Afternoon lessons were beginning in the outdoor arena; staff were fetching horses in from the fields; a lorry arrived to deliver something.

Soon, when no one was about, Amber could slip away to Thornby Manor.

But she had reckoned without Sam. It seemed like every five minutes Sam came to check on her. As if she had nothing better to do, thought Amber.

The next time Sam appeared, Amber said she was going to lie down in her tent for a while.

"That's fine," said Sam. "I was just coming to tell you I've got to take a pony up to the manor. I won't be long."

Amber sprang to her feet. "Can I come with you?" she asked.

Sam looked surprised.

"I think a walk might do me good," said Amber.

She couldn't believe her luck.

It was only when they were on their way that she thought perhaps it wasn't such a good idea. How could she do anything private with Sam there? They'd arrive, hand over Oscar, then turn around and leave. There would be no chance to talk to anyone. And Amber wanted to talk. She couldn't just give up. She wanted to tell whoever it was that owned Oscar what she thought of people who got rid of animals when they couldn't be bothered with them any more. Because as far as she could see, there was absolutely nothing wrong with Oscar.

She had just decided to ask Sam if she knew anything about him when a tractor passed, tooted its horn, and pulled up further along the main street.

Sam seemed flustered. She pushed the lead-rope into Amber's hands. "Look," she said, pointing to the lane across the way. "Thornby Manor's up there. Take the pony, tell them we're sorry about the mix-ups. I've just got to do something. Come back and wait for me here."

She sped off towards the tractor. A lad had jumped down.

Amber walked up the lane to the manor. If only she could keep walking. If only she could take Oscar somewhere truly safe. She felt like a traitor. How could she be taking him back to the very place from which she'd rescued him?

The boy was waiting at the manor gates.

"I'm glad it's you," he said. "I hoped it would be."

"I haven't got long," said Amber. There were so many questions she wanted to ask.

"Is Oscar yours?" she began. "Because, if so, why? Why are you letting him be killed?"

The boy flinched. "Look," he said. He didn't offer to take Oscar. "Could you put him in his field? We can talk as we go."

Amber explained about Sam.

"I'll be as quick as I can," promised the boy. His name was Hugh, he told her. No, Oscar didn't belong to him. Oscar belonged to his sister.

"Emma's my twin," he said. "She lives in Austria now, with my mother. When my parents split up, Emma went with Mum, I stayed here with my father." He paused. "I didn't have a choice."

Amber let Oscar into his field and came back to the gate.

"Of course, Oscar had to stay too," Hugh continued. "I promised Emma I'd look after him; but I don't ride and, well, I'm not very good with horses." He grimaced. "No, that's not true. They scare me to death! My father's never accepted how I feel. Then, last week, he exploded, said he was fed up keeping a pony that no one rode, and, well, you know the rest, don't you? I saw you stand up to those boys. That time when they were throwing stones." He broke off. "I know I should have tried to stop them."

"Was it you who followed us?" said Amber. "That night when Molly and I rescued Oscar?"

Hugh nodded. "I couldn't sleep," he said, "and when I saw what you were doing, I was so relieved, I can't tell you."

"So there's nothing wrong with Oscar?" asked Amber.

"Nothing," said Hugh.

"Right," said Amber. She told him about Jen. "I'm sure she'd be happy to talk some sense into your father."

Hugh brightened. "When can she come?" he asked. "My father's back tonight. He's been away on business all week."

"Oh, but Jen's away!" said Amber, suddenly remembering. "And if we don't stop them tonight, Oscar will be killed. Can't you talk to your dad? At least persuade him to wait until Jen gets back."

Hugh shook his head. "You don't know what my father's like," he said. "When he finds out Oscar is still here..."

Amber grinned. "What if Oscar isn't here?" she said. "He's been around a bit this

week. But there's one place he hasn't been."
It had occurred to her on the way home
from the hack but she'd never thought she
might have to use it. "One place where I'm
certain he'd be safe," she added.

Hugh stared. "I can't think of anywhere."

Amber told him.

Hugh's jaw dropped. "Are you sure?"

"I've read about it," said Amber. "No one,
not even your father, could touch him."

A voice called from the main street.

"I've got to go," said Amber. Quickly she
outlined her plan. "Cross everything!" she
said.

One last chance, she thought, as she ran
down the lane to meet Sam.

Later that evening, Amber managed to get Molly on her own. At first, Molly didn't want even to listen, never mind do anything.

"I just want you to give Jen a message the minute she gets here," said Amber. "She's definitely coming back tomorrow. Sam told me."

Molly was still worried. And she was panic-stricken when Amber told her what message to give.

"You'll be where?! She won't believe me. I can't."

"You're the only person I trust," pleaded Amber. "You used to be my friend."

Molly flushed. "I still am."

"You needn't say anything about your part," said Amber.

At last Molly agreed.

At six o'clock the following morning, Amber was back at Thornby Manor. Hugh was waiting at the gates, carrying a bulging hay-net.

"Provisions," he explained.

"For ten ponies by the look of it!" said Amber.

They went up the lane to catch Oscar. It didn't take long. Oscar trotted over as soon as he saw them.

"There's a short cut we can take," said Hugh as they set off. "So we don't have to go through the village."

"Right," said Amber. She didn't want to go back past the manor. She only wanted to meet Hugh's father when she was good and ready.

Within minutes they were going through a gate – a bit of a squeeze for Oscar – and up a narrow path between ancient gravestones.

"What if it's locked?" said Amber suddenly.

Hugh produced a key. "My mother used to be in charge of the flower rota," he explained.

It was a huge key. But then it was a gigantic door. Hugh opened it while Amber persuaded Oscar into the porch. He wasn't very happy at first to leave the sunlight, but then Hugh came back with the hay-net and, little by little, they eased Oscar through. They were in the church!

Inside, it was cool and quiet. Hugh tied the hay-net to a pew, but there was nowhere to secure Oscar. Anyway, Amber wanted to hold him, talk to him, reassure him. He was understandably jittery in his new surroundings.

"Are you sure about this sanctuary thing?" said Hugh.

"Certain," said Amber. "Anyone can claim sanctuary in a church. No one can harm them." She grinned. "This might possibly be the first time a pony has claimed sanctuary though!"

They heard footsteps approaching. Hugh went to the door. "It's the vicar," he said. "Let's hope he knows about sanctuary."

The vicar was, by turns, amazed, kind, understanding, and finally exasperated, when Amber refused to take Oscar out of his church.

"Not until Hugh's father assures us that no harm will come to him," said Amber firmly.

"I've left a message for him to come here," explained Hugh. "We feel that if he promises in church, it'll mean something."

"But I have a Pram Service at nine thirty," said the vicar. "I can't have a pony in church!"

Hugh promised they'd be long gone by then.

But when the first prams and pushchairs began to arrive, there was still no sign of Hugh's father.

The service began.

At the front of the church, children pivoted in their seats and craned their necks to see the pony. Those who were old enough to talk kept demanding to see him, to stroke him. The vicar's jolly story went unheard. In the end, he took them all to the back of the church and told them the story of St Francis of Assisi and how he had loved all animals.

"Especially ponies," said one little girl.

"Especially ponies," the vicar agreed.

When the service ended and all the children had been persuaded to leave, quiet was restored.

"I can't think why my father hasn't come," said Hugh. "The message I left was clear and to the point."

"Maybe he's decided not to," said Amber.

As the morning wore on she began to worry about Jen. By now, surely Molly had given her the message asking her to come to the church to meet Hugh's father. But suppose Jen hadn't returned?

Amber felt her plan falling to pieces around her.

The vicar came and went.

A few visitors arrived, looking not a little surprised to see a pony. "Is it a tradition?" one asked. "Is it a special day?"

Neither Amber nor Hugh felt like explaining. They were beginning to feel hungry. "I wish I'd brought provisions for *us*," said Hugh.

The church clock struck two.

Pony Camp will almost have finished, thought Amber. Rosettes and certificates will have been given out. The end-of-camp gymkhana will be about to start.

"Do you think we should go home?" asked Hugh.

"No," said Amber firmly. "We've got to stick it out."

Two more visitors entered the church. Amber braced herself for questions. But these visitors didn't ask any. They simply fell upon Hugh and Oscar as if they'd known them all their lives.

As soon as he could, Hugh turned to Amber. "This is my mother," he said, "and my sister, Emma."

"We knew something was wrong when you didn't phone," said Emma, after Hugh had told them the whole story. "We phone or text each other every day," she explained to Amber.

"I couldn't bear to tell you," said Hugh, "knowing there was nothing I could do."

"And then along came Amber!" said Emma.

"I don't think Father's coming," said Hugh.

"Oh, yes, he is," said his mother. "I've been in touch. He'll be here."

A jazzy tune suddenly filled the church. "Sorry," said Amber. "My phone."

It was Molly. "Just to tell you Jen's on her way," she said. "Oh and Jack won the Cup. You got a Special for hacking though. Are you all right?"

Amber smiled. "Yes," she said. "So far."

Jen, Hugh's father, several ladies laden with flowers, and the vicar all arrived together. The church seemed crowded. Everyone began to talk at once. Except Hugh.

Eventually, the vicar made himself heard. He addressed the whole company but Hugh's father in particular. "If you could just clear up this whole matter as quickly as possible," he said, "I'd be very grateful."

"It's just a lot of fuss about nothing," said Hugh's father.

"Nothing!" cried Amber. "It's not nothing. You planned to have this pony killed!"

Hugh's father laughed. "Wherever did you get that idea?" he said.

Amber was furious. "How dare you deny it?" she shouted. "I heard it with my own ears!"

Hugh's father was unruffled. "From whom?" he enquired.

"A gang of boys," she said.

"Oh, well," scoffed Hugh's father. "It *must* be true then."

Hugh spoke. "But I thought you told Bill—" he began.

His father looked at him pityingly. "I merely told Bill to get rid of the animal. Sell it, not kill it."

There was a stunned silence. "And that's still what I intend to do," he added. He turned to the vicar. "I think that just about clears it up. Now, if you'll excuse me."

No one spoke as he walked out of the church. Emma was crying.

"I'm so sorry, Emma," said Hugh.

"Nonsense," said Hugh's mother. "It's not your fault. Anyway it's not going to happen.

Oscar belongs to Emma." And she marched everyone out of the church, including Oscar.

Emma was still crying as they walked back to the manor. "I know what will happen as soon as we've gone," she said to Amber. "And you can't keep saving Oscar."

Amber looked ahead to where Emma's mother and Jen were deep in conversation.

"Cross everything!" she said. If only Jen would buy Oscar for the riding school...

"Amber, could you put Oscar in his stable?" said Emma's mother, when they reached the manor. "We just have a few things to sort out. We won't be long."

When Amber was called inside, everything was settled. Oscar would still belong to Emma, but he would go to live at the riding school.

"That's wonderful!" cried Amber.

"But he will need exercising," said Emma's mother. "Daily. Emma would like you to do it, Amber. Jen says you're perfectly capable and that you come up to help most days anyway. Would you mind taking that on?"

Mind? Amber's head spun. To be able to ride Oscar every day! She couldn't speak.

"He's fun, but he doesn't do anything silly, if you know what I mean," said Emma. "And he's good in traffic. You can go hacking on him easily. I think you'll enjoy him."

Amber found her voice. "Oh, I will!" she said.

"Good. That's settled then," said Emma's mother. "Now, we think it's best that you take him straight away."

Amber rode Oscar to his new home. Here we go again! she thought. But this time, she was *riding* Oscar. In broad daylight – with nothing to hide! Down the main street, past the pub, past the playground where a gang of boys was playing football, and on, under the trees, to the riding school.

Jumping Beany

June Crebbin

It's Pony Day at Merryfield Hall Riding School and, for the first time ever, Dad has promised to come and watch Amber jump. Everything will be perfect … as long as Amber gets to ride her favourite pony, Beany. But Donna wants to ride Beany too – and, as the jumping competition gets closer, it looks like she'll go to any lengths to get her own way!

When she was ten years old, Katrina Picket woke Merlin.

It was quite by accident – she'd had no intention of doing any such thing. But it was fortunate for everyone in England that she did. They didn't know, of course. The whole thing had to be hushed up. Most people thought it was a particularly inventive party for the Queen's jubilee. And as for the dragon and the exploding fireball – they were explained away as impressive special effects.

But Katrina, and the Prime Minister, knew different...

"Fast-moving fun." *The Scotsman*

If you've enjoyed reading this book, look out for...

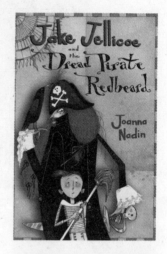

Short novels for fluent readers